A Shaken Bible

A Shaken Bible

by Steve Hanson

Beyond Criticism Editions

BOILER HOUSE PRESS

For my dear one. All or none.
Everyone under the sun.

Contents

Preface

The prose-poem at the core of this work is a feast of rich, reworked, largely seventeenth century English. One might enjoy it simply for the sheer surface sumptuousness of the language, to be dipped into.

But it is also a sacramental enactment of negative theology.

It is an experiment in a new genre; revelling in the potential of the word-processor, as its instrument. For the most part a literary collage, it begins as an act of homage to the Authorized Version of the Bible, which it takes as its basis. However, it bids to revivify what it draws from the Authorized Version, by mixing it up with other texts and rendering it, in the process, really very strange.

The work began with a reading of Gillian Rose's book, *The Broken Middle*. Under this title, Rose identifies the most sacred truth with a patient, negotiative occupancy of that 'middle' most buffeted, to the point of being most 'broken', by all manner of contradictory moral claims. The Authorized Version originated, essentially, as the fundamental sacred text at the 'middle' of a newly self-conscious Englishness: the final definitive replacement, in that role, for the Latin of the Vulgate.

Hanson's work is itself a systematic buffeting, and breaking-open, of this 'middle'. He has taken a word-processor to it; respectfully, worried and worked it; as it were, testing it, to reveal something of its inner strength, half-hidden by comfortable familiarity.

He sets out his procedure. First, he removed the semi-colons from the Authorized Version; then the numbers. Then he re-ordered the sequence of books, starting from Amos as, historically speaking, in a sense the first.

For Amos is the book that actually sets the basic problem with which, in one way or another, most of the rest of the biblical writers are wrestling. Namely, once again: how to build a community – a functioning 'middle', one might say – which will truly be faithful to the most intransigent principles of 'justice and righteousness', and yet still cohere, even though the intransigence of those infinite demands is forever threatening to break it apart.

Next he quite drastically shortened the text, keeping only what immediately spoke to him; and simply excising, for instance, the all too familiar and ambiguous actual word 'God'. Into what remained, he inserted other voices. Notably, texts of Abiezer Coppe the Ranter; other dissident writers from the English Civil War; and William Blake: biblically minded rejecters of the Anglican establishment.

To add another deep sort of echo, he also threw a few fragments from the Epic of Gilgamesh, for example, into the stew. And, in an ultimate violent gesture of negation, he re-ordered the whole in sections named after the ten months of the French revolutionary calendar. Yes, there is a sublated fury here.

Then he rendered it into Yorkshire/Lancashire dialect. Hanson himself comes from Walsden, a Pennine valley village, on the way to Manchester from Todmorden. The dialect of this area is, as he puts it, 'a slave language, like Cockney or Patois': historically, it is a language of Industrial Revolution mill-workers. Nowadays, one may still hear it, among their descendants, surviving, more or less astray, in a post-industrial world.

This procedure reflects the political 'brokenness' of the 'middle' which the Authorized Version was once designed to occupy.

First, and most obviously, it has been broken by the secularization of the culture; by the sheer proliferation of religious, and overtly irreligious, diversity. You hear the resonant old words, and you know there's no way back to that lost world.

But, second, it has also been broken by class conflict between the national elite – the class who, in the seventeenth century, actually spoke the language of the Authorized Version – and the other, geographically more fragmented classes, speaking their various dialects. All of which are represented here, collectively by the particular dialect of the Pennine mill-towns.

And, third, it has been broken by the establishment's failure adequately to respond to the prophetic Amos-like challenge chiefly represented, here, by Coppe and Blake.

Clearly, no single sacred text could nowadays do the civil-religious job for which the Authorized Version was originally intended. And yet, the basic problem remains: how, then, is the 'broken middle' most truthfully to be occupied, in our world? It is a matter of honestly acknowledging the full 'brokenness' of the context; even whilst still holding fast to the project of a genuine, universally 'mediating' thoughtfulness. Indeed: holding fast to it, very much, as a sacred aspiration. Hanson's work, poetically, evokes that abiding problem.

There have been a great many popularizing attempts to render the Bible into one sort or another of 'ordinary' modern English. They have all, of course, been promoted as attempts to make it more accessible; easier to read. But here, in A Shaken Bible, the point is, we have the exact opposite.

Here we have a deliberate attempt to render the text – that is, what is still left of it – more difficult to read. In a certain sense, even, as difficult as possible.

Or, rather: here we have an attempt to show the true difficulty of the text, precisely in all its potential depth, as divine revelation, despite everything. Here, easy understanding is balked.

And the aim, I guess, is that in the process every last trace of glib, cliché-ridden or kitsch-inflected interpretation is sieved away. So that all that then shines forth – like a few grains of gold, remaining – is the pure element of the sublime.

That is what I mean when I say that this text is a sacramental enactment of negative theology. Much of it I do not understand; but never mind. God does not primarily demand understanding. I sense that it enshrines sheer moral longing, and that is enough. In its curious, eloquently frustrating, and uncanny way I guess, that, to those who have ears to hear, it speaks significant truth.

—*Andrew Shanks*

Warning

This book began as a collage. I attended a conference on the work of Gillian Rose with my friend Mark Rainey at the University of Durham. It was a fraught event, it troubled me. When I returned home, I strategically began to process a text version of the King James Bible of 1611.

First, I took all the semi-colons out. Then I took all the numbers out. The semi-colons set up many of the phrases in the bible as questions, and then answered them for you. The numbers were and are the juridical numbers of legal process. Immediately I realised that I had a very different document: The form of language and its content are not separable.

I then re-ordered the books beginning with the oldest one, historically, which is the book of Amos the prophet. I then edited out everything that did not feel like it belonged to the sweaty, disturbing quality of contemporary life.

The word 'god' was the first to go. Then whole books and sections were removed as I swept over this text again and again.

I began to insert the heretical and dissident voices from the era, Abiezer Coppe the ranter and William Blake for instance. I went over and over this material, removing multiple instances of single words from the entire document in one move, but not adding any writing of my own. I eventually re-ordered the resulting material in sections relating to the ten months of the French revolutionary calendar.

I had enough material for six sections. I then went over this material repeatedly, processing it each time. When this process slowed to a near halt, I suddenly realised that I needed to 'slang up' the material. To put it in the mouths of the neo-proletariat of the globalised world. The hourly slaves.

I then removed all the pointless double letters, to make the language as lean as a starving refugee.

I added own my Yorkshire/Lancashire border tongue, which is a slave language, like Cockney or Patois. These languages emerge from biblical language, but make themselves minor languages, to evade the surveillance of the master-tongue, the major language of the major discourse.

When this was done, I had a new language. This new language immediately took over me and my project: I stopped writing it and it began to write me. This was an important shift. Rather than processing found material, I was now writing, but I was writing through those transformed and resurrected voices from the past. Not literally, but *literally*.

I then went through the whole document again and again, as this transformed ghost writer of a new tongue. This is what you hold in your hands. It is important to state upfront that this is a difficult work, but I want you to walk into it unarmed and unprepared.

This is a warning.

—*Steve Hanson*

A Shaken Bible

His pen, his scalpel cut.
The writer of the Zohar surgically drew blood,
pulsing, from the unseen circulation
of the stars, gathered in a cup
the words, the homesick sparks.

The grave split open, the alphabet arose,
each letter was an angel, each a crystal shard,
each held refracted droplets dating from Creation.

These sang. And there, within, glowed
ruby, jacinth, lapis lazuli,
so many scattered seedlings
not yet stone.

And night, the blackest tiger,
roared; and wounded day
lay writhing there,
in pools of light.

The shining was a mouth tight shut.
An aura, only, showed God hid within the soul.

—Nelly Sachs (trans., Andrew Shanks)

I. PRIMIDI

i. Leaving

Hear this word, ye kine, that opres the poor. Ther is a famin i' the land. Not a famin of bred, nor a thirst for water, but of hearin. At five double hours, the darknes was dense, it did not alow him to sea.

He leves ther a'ter, ther the venturer leves the bludied. Ypocrites. Neocrites. After dippin the sop, he leves an sekes the troubled priests i' the church o' the tent mak'r. One folo'ed to draw him back. I was that one. He wud not draw back, but hav me seke refuge with him, that I mite take wot burned in his hart. An we gane'd sanctuary. An we sat. An he spoke.

And they shal wander from sea to sea, an from the north ee'n tut sarth. They shal run to an fro to seke an shal not find. Hear this, oh ye that swalow up an crush the neady, mayk the poor to fail, falsifying balances by deceit.

Wot time is this, that we may buy the poor for silver, an the neady for a pair of shoes, yea, an sel the refuse of the wheat?

Nay. He wil take yu away with hooks, an yewer posterity with fishhooks. Yur treading is pon the poor, an ye take from him burthens of wheat. Yu hav built harses of 'ewen stown, but ye shal not dwel in them, not one o' yer. Ye'v planted vinyards, but yu shal not drink, not one.

I kno' yewer manifold transgresions. They aflict the just, they take a bribe, an they turn aside the poor i' the gate from thier rites. Shal the prudent keap silence in that evil time? Seke gud, an not evil, that ye may live. They shal cawl the husbandman to mornin', an such as ar skilful, of lamentation to wailing, an more. Yet the onion has many layers, an' c'n'c. Think on this.

But stil let judgment run down as waters thus, an rite'ousnes as a mitey stream, on they that lie 'pon beds of ivory, an stretch themsels pon thier carches, an eat the lambs aht the flock, an the calves aht the midst o' the stawl.

Not enuf salt fer thee tears hear.

They that chant to the sound of the viol, an invent of themsels instruments of music, that drink the wine in bowls, an anoint themsels with chief ointments, they ar not grieved fer the afliction.

I hayt, I despise yewer feast days an solemn asemblies. Tho ye ofer meats, I wil not ascepter them. Neeth'r wil I regard the peace oferings of yewer fat beasts. Take thou away from me the noise of thy songs, for I wil not hear the melody of thy viols. Fancy music fer few ere's.

The erth wil darken i' the clere day. I wil turn yewer feasts into morning, an awl yur songs into lamentation, an I wil bring baldnes 'pon ev'ry hed, an I wil mayk it as the morning of an only son, an the end therof as a day of sharp biting. Therfor now shal they go captive, an the banquet of them that stretched themsels shal be removed to no fancy musics. Tho they dig into hel, thence shal mine hand take them. Tho they climb up, thence wil I bring them down.

I wil set mine eyes 'pon them for evil, an not for gud. Tho they hide from my site in the botom of the sea - tho' they belong ther - thence wil I comand the snake bitch Ananke, an she shal bite them awl. I wil give yewer skuls a clene nes of teath, I hav smiten yu with blasting an mildew, an yewer gardens.

An yewer gardens.

And since it has bene writen in stown an the fragments sold for the myriad, that 'the mountains shal drop swete wine an awl the hils shal melt, an they shal build the waste citis an inhabit them, an they shal plant vinyards, an drink the wine therof.'

Thus shal I declare this mere tales and talk, with mine own tales an-a talkin. If yer gee it aht yer ave to be ale tek it. I hav tek'n it fer awl my life.

'An I wil plant pon thier land, an they shal no more be pul'd up aht thier land?'

The land doth not merely lie, tis fil'd with lies as such. As fish to thier stewponds. And I said Roar, the habitations of the poor shal morn, rivers swel an banks drain. For threa transgresions, an for four, I wil not turn away the punishment, because they hav threshed with threshing instruments. I wil send a fire of spirit into the harse to devower the palayces.

Because he did pursue his broth'r, an did cast away awl pity, an his angr did tear perpetualy, an he kept his wrath forev'r. These ar Roman, whippin times. The day burns like an oven.

My deare one. Awl or non. Ev'ryone under the sun. I hav changed in a moment, in the twinkling of an eye. No more thea an them, nor I. The sea, the erth, yea, awl things ar giving up thier ded. An awl things that e'r wer, ar, or shal be, visible. That sin an transgresion be finished?

Nay, only tales of the losing and finding of the self, for thowsands of years. 'For whoe'r wud save his life will lose it, but whoev'r loses his life will find it', or 'be transformed by the renewal of yur mind' and lo, 'he is a new creation, the old has passed away', an behold, 'the new has com.'

Tales anna talkin. Such wer the tales an talk of the day. Such tales and talk.

ii. Warning

And further he spake, this venturer, i' the church o' the tent mak'r. This is a warning warning warning warning warning. Oh, I was among awl the Demons in hel, in thier most hideous hue. Sin began to lie at my door. I hath bene infected wit' plague. Yet tis the plague of swareing after scrupulous self-restraint. I was in private, an secret fasting often. Tears wer my drink, ash and shit my meat.

My hairs wer grown like eagle feathers, 'ands as bird claws. Ther was a man, grim, face like a bird, hands of lion's paws, with claws of eagle talons, took hold of my hair, overpow'rd me. I struck him but he sprang back like a skipping-rope. He struck me and capsised me like a raft. I went under for a ful season.

Now was I com up in spirit thro' the flaming. I knew nothing but purenes, inocensy an rite'ousnes. It is meat an drink to an angel to sware, a joy to curse like a Demon. I was fil'd brim ful with intoxicating wine, an I drank it of, ee'n the dregs.

I hav insinuated sev'ral blasphemous opinions ee'en the eyes o' the hundreds.

Thows who talk only omnipresence an esence, hav bene sore ofended by me.

Yet I spoke truth contrary to eror, but thows days ar ended, as he sets up a brazen serpent wen he pleas'th, an it grinds to powd'r wen it pleas'th. An yet he saith 'thou shalt do no adultery', an 'fly fornication', an yet further he saith, 'get thea children', of fornication. Thier harses go'th on the adultery an regular. Phanes hear me. I hav bene a long while cloth'd i' filthy garments an hath lain ay i' the chan'l o' the streat. Ev'ry one that paced me by cast dirt pon me, an I hav lain stil. Aye sea it bet'r in this shit chan'l than in thier palayces.

I hav patiently an silently heard myself acounted the fath'r of mischief, son of hewers, an the awthor of erors.

These erors broached, an wer they bodies, I wud dash thier brains an bones agin the hard stowns that line the streat, an in not one part of the streat do they not.

Ignorance, weaknes, mistake, misaprehension an misunderstanding hath wasted an uterly undun thea. That I hav scarce clothes to hang on my back.

The dark hides not, but the night shines like the day. No rid'l, this.

And under awl this teror an amazement, ther was a spark of transcendent, transplendent, unspekeable glory wich surviv'd, an sustain'd itself, triumphing, exulting an exalting itself, above awl the fiends. An confounding awl the bleaknes an darknes - ye must take it on these terms, tho it is infinitely beyond expresion - pon this the life I was taken aht my bodi for a season, as if a man with a great brush dip'd in whiting should with one stroke swipe a picture from its canvas.

After a while, breath an life was returned to form agane. Wher'pon I clerely saw distinction, diversity, variety. Complexity folded up in unity. An it hath bene my song many times since, within an without, unity, universality - universality, unity. Eternal Majesty, an' c'n'c. An inlet into the Land of Promise an a gate into the ensuing Discourse, worthy of serious consideration.

And at this vision, a most strong, gloriuss voice utr'd these words, 'the spirits of just men may'd flesh'. The spirits with whom I had as absolute, clere, ful comunion, an in a more twofold familiar way, than ev'r I had outwardly with my dearest an nereest. The visions an revelations of eternal, invisible almitines wer stretched aht pon me, within me, for the spayce of days an nights without intermision.

The time wud fail if I wud tel awl, but amongst thows various voices that wer utered within, these wer some: Blud, blud, wher, wher, pon the Ypocritical holy hart.

This is a warning warning warning warning warning.

Oh, anoth'r thus. Venge'ance, venge'ance, avenge'ance, plagues pon the inhabitants of the Erth. Fire, fire, sublime fireworks pon awl that bow not to eternal, universal love. I'l recover, recover my wul, my flax, my money. Declare, declare. Fret thou not the faces of any. I am in thea, a munition of rocks an' c'n'c.

Go up to London, to London, that great Citi, write write write. Behold I writ, an lo a hand was sent to me, an a book was within, wich this fleshly hand wud hav to put wings to befor the time. Wher'pon it was snatched aht mine hand an thrust into my mouth, an I ate it up, an fil'd my bowels wi it, wher it wer biting as wormwood, an lay broilin an burning in my stomach, til I brought it forth in this form.

And now I send it flying to thea, with mine hart an awl. I inform yu that I overturn, overturn, overturn. As the bishops hav had thier turn, overturn. Soe yur turn shal be next, by wot name or title soev'r. Great ones must bow to the poorest peasants or else they shal rue for it. This very day.

Yet this hand wich now writes ne'r shed one drop of an-yone's blud. I am frea from the blud of awl, awl things ar reconciled to me. An more justice, rite'ousnes, sister, an sincerity shining in thows low dung holes, as they ar es-teamed, than in their stars. I com not with any metal, but lay the powd'r of the spirit, twenty barels ful i' the celar o' the livin bein, as it wer with one blast, sudenly an barba-rously, to blow up an tear in pieces this heiresy of the hart.

Thows that hav admir'd, adored, idolised, magnified, set yu up, fought for yu, ventured guds an gud name, limb an life for yu, shal cease from yu.

Yu shal not at awl be acounted for, not one of yu. Ye sturdy oak, fire, fire, who bow not down befor universal love, whose service is perfect freadom.

Remember, remember yur for-runner puting down the mit-ey from thier setes, exalting them of low degra. I repete, I repete mesen with reason, as I repeal. As yu wil see, and then to sea, an c 'n' c.

Let not for yer own sakes the beast within or without yu, ministers, moneylenders, workmasters, roten parsons, swo-len lecturers, who for thier own base ends, to maintain thier pride an pomp, an to fil thier own paunches an purses, hav bene the chief instruments of awl horid abominations. Hel-ish, cruel, demonish Ratio, persecutions in this Nation wich cry for venge'ance. For yur own sakes, I say, let them not be-witch yu or charm yewer ears. To hear them say, these things shal not befawl yu, shal not be fulfil'd pon Yu, but pon The Oth'r, hethen princes, an' c'n'c. If any of them should, thro subtlety, for their own base ends, creap into the mistery an tel yu such, then thows words ar to be taken in mistery. They only point aht an inward, not an ahtward leveling.

This is 'Evil to him that Evil thinks', for thou an awl thy rev'rend divines, so-caled, ar ignorant of this one thing, that sin an transgresion be finished. It is a mere rid'l that they, with awl their human learning, can nev'r read.

Believe them not. For this honour, nobility, gentility, propriety, superfluity is, an most strangely without contra diction, the fath'r of helish horid pride, arogance, haughtines, loftines, malice an murther. Awl manner of wickednes an impiety. Yea, the cause of awl the blud that ev'r hath bene shed, from the blud of the rite'ous Abel to the blud of the last Leveler shot to deeth, an ev'r on. The root of the wronged on awl sides, in the so-caled Lands of the Holy. For ther ar no sides in the Rite'ous Citi, an yet sack an sucour hav bene as one.

Wot mak ye of this? Now as I live I am com to mayk inquisition. By the fire of the New Crosing Turnpike, at the town of D'th Murther, in the cutch at the Mouth of the River, in the Mid Lands, in Derby, Notingham an Lincoln Shire, in awl of the Great Citis an Unplayses alike.

For in any playse iniquity doth dwel, an in spite of thier subtlety an diligence, thier craft an cruelty of hel an erth, this leveling shal up.

But we scorn to fite for owt. We wud as hapily be ded drunk ev'ry day of the weak, an lie with hewers in the market playse, an acount these as gud actions, as taking the poor, abused, enslaved's money from 'er, who is almost ev'ry-wher undun an' squeazed to the deeth. Not soe much as that plaguey, unsuportable, helish burthen an opresion of tithes taken off her shoulders. Notwithstanding awl is honesty, fidelity, taxes, frea quarter, petitioning, an' c'n'c, for the same. We had rather starve, I say, than take away money from her or him, for the kiling of.

Nay, if we mite hav the pay of the chief executor, an a gud fat parsonage or two besides, we wud scorn to be gunmen, or fite, with thows mostly carnal weapons, for owt, or agin any-one, or for ower livings. My words.

But for my labore, I hav bene plagued an tormented be-yond expresion. Soe that now I had rather behold one pouring aht the plagues, cursing, an teechin oth'rs to curse bit'rly, an tearin the hair of his hed like the mad, cursin an making oth'rs fawl a-swareing, than hear a zealous no-tionist pray, preach or exercise. Let it be how it wil. These so-caled Levelers yu mostly hayt'd, tho in ahtward decl'ra-tions, yu owned thier tenets as yur own principle. Rot.

Once more, kno' that blasting beyond words is not my prin-ciple. I only pronounce as I durst. Soe mostly, yu hayt me, tho in ahtward decl'rations yu profesy me, an seam to own me, more than a thousand whom yu despise, who ar nereer the spirit than yewer selves. I spit in yewer faces.

London, London, my bowels ar roled tog'ther in me for thea, an my compasions within ar kindled. Befor many of thine inhabitants' faces, among oth'r strange exploits, beheld me fawl down flat, at the feat of adicts, beg'rs an the sick. Resigning up my money to them, being sev'ral times over-emptied of money that ah yad not one penny left, an yet have recruited me a-gane. With hand fiercely stretched aht, hat cocked up, eyes set to sparkle aht, an with a mit-ey loud voice, charged of the myriad voltages. I hav proclaimed the notable day to one thousand men an women of the greatest rank, an many notorious, debauched, swareing, roistering, roaring an oth'r wild sparks of the gentry, thro the streats of the Great Citi.

But many notorious vile ones in the esteam of men, yea, of great quality among men, doth tremble, for they kno' not wot aye sea.

The Demon in yu roared aht who was tormented to some purpose, tho not befor his time. He showed both 'is fangs an paws ther an wud hav torn me to pieces an hav me eaten. Thier pride, envy, malice, arogance, an' c'n'c, poured aht like a river of mercury. Crying aht, 'a blasphemer', at length threatening, 'a Blasphemer, away with him.' Let it be how it wil. For we ar awl born at adventure, and shall hereafter be as tho' we had nev'r bene, the breath in our nostrils as smoke, a lit'l spark in the movin of our hart.

But I wil spit a flame of tongues, because they hav ripened then ripped up the woman with child, that they mite enlarge thier borders. Thier lies caused them to er. Shouting in the day of batle, a tempest in the day of the whirlin wind. He that is courageous among the mitey shal flea away naked in that day.

Publish in the palayces, asemble thyselves. Behold the great tumults in the midst therof, an the opresed therof. For they kno' not to do rite, who stor up violence an robery in thier palayces. Seke gud, not evil, that yu may live.

Tho neeth'r wil I ascept the peace oferings of yewer fat beasts. I wil search an take them aht, ee'n tho they hide at the botom of the sea. I wil set mine eyes on them for evil, not gud, an then we wil build the waste citis an inhabit them, plant vinyards, drink the wine, mayk gardens, an eat the fruit. Thows rid'ls, stil.

And yet yu fly as if yu nest among the stars! An soe yu wil plumet. If robbers came by night, for how cut off yu hav may'd yurself, with land an gates. Wud they steal only 'til they had enuf? If the grape-gather'rs came, wud they leve some grapes? Did yu do such in yewer time?

Both sides may confer that the hethen drink continualy. Swalow down then an be as tho they had not bene.

But the men who wer at peace with yu hav deceived yu, an prevailed agin yu. They eat yur bred as they casualy lay wounds in yu, ther is no understanding in them.

Yu should not hav laid hands on them in the day of thier calamity. Waited at the border to cut of thier escape. Grasing over thows that remained. Wot yu hav dun wil be dun to yu, thy reward shal return pon thine own hed. Yet wot dost thou think of this? This warning.

iii. Violation

And soe I rose up to flea from mine own path, an cried by reason of afliction, an was flung into hel, an then agane aht the bely of hel. For the trew Violation is the Violation of the self thus. Grievous corection lies for him that forsakes his own path. They that observe lyin' vanities forsake thier own mercy.

I say agane, grievous corection lies in wait for him that forsakes his own, strange, dificult path, of myriad complexity. Tho observers shal rare understand it, ee'n thows thou lovest dear.

This shal be my gilt, not fingers ful of blud.

Yet I wil prophesy unto thea of wine an of strong drink, an of stronger, wich shal ee'n be the prophet of this peple who hayt the gud, an love the evil.

Who pluck thier skin from off them, an their flesh from thier bones, who eat the flesh of the peple, an flay their skin from off them.

They break thier bones, chop them in pieces, as for the pot, an as flesh within the cauldron. This is their stock.

Yet be slow to angr, an great in pow'r, an not at awl quick to damn the wicked. Yur way is of the whirlwind an in the storm, an its clouds ar the dust of yur feat. The feat of him that bringes gud tidings, that publishes peace, perform thy vows. For the wicked shal noe more pass thro thea, he is uterly cut off. While they be folden to th' gither as thorns, an while they ar drunken as the Thames, they shal be devowered as stubble, fuly dry. The emptiers hav emptied them aht.

The lion did tear in pieces enuf for his whelps, an strangled suficient for his lioneses, an fil'd his holes with prey. Woe to the bludy Citi! It is awl ful of lies an robery. The prey departes not the noise of the whip, an the noise of the ratling of wheals, nor of the prancing. Ther is no end of thier prancing, nor of thier corpses, they stumbl pon their corpses.

They drop from thier mouthes an thier arses. Because of the profligacy of the wel-favoured, the masters of witchcrafts, that seles nations thro' profligacy, an families thro' wizard-ry, an' c'n'c.

This is the Citi of wich I speke. I wil shew thy nations thy na-kednes, an thy spirits thy real shame. I wil cast abominable filth pon thea, an mak thea vile, an wil set thea as a stock. Thea an thine. Thy crowned ar as the locusts, thy nobles shal dwel in the ash an in the shit. The Lawe is slacked, an judgment doth nev'r go forth, for the wicked doth compas about the rite'ous. Ther' for wrong judgment procead'th.

But the burthen. Why shew me iniquity, an cause me to be-hold grievance? For spoiling an violence ar befor me, an ther ar thows that raise up strife an contention. Why mak me sea, wher oth'rs be born or ar gladly blind? Most yet merely see.

I sea its infinite gradations. I sea as the sea. I canot do oth'r. Therfor I wil not turn away tho' it cause me grief without rest. Thus grievous corection lies in wait for her or him that forsakes his or her strange dificult path, of myriad complex-ity, in them as for me.

Behold ye among the hethen, an regard, an wonder marve-lously, for I wil work a work in yur days wich ye wil not be-lieve in that bit'r an hasty nation.

To posess the dweling playses that ar not thiers. They ar teri-ble an dreadful, thier judgment an dignity shal procead of themsels. They travel swifter than the leopards, more fierce than the ee'nin wolves, an they spred themsels. They shal fly as the eagle that hastens to eat.

They shal com awl for violence, thier faces shal sup up as the east wind, an they shal gather the captivity as the sand, an they shal scof at the kings, an the princes shal be a scorn unto them, they shal deride ev'ry stronghold, for they shal heap burning coals of shame on thier heds, an take it.

Consider this.

Thou art of purer eyes than to behold evil, an canst not look on iniquity, nor holdest thy tongue wen the wicked devoweres the man that is more rite'ous, my love, an mayk'st men as the fishes of the sea, as of the creeping things. They take up awl of them with the angle, they catch them in thier net, an gather them in their drag, therfor they rejoice an ar glad.

Yet how bonny an deliteful yu ar, my love, my awl.

So write the vision, an mak it plain 'pon tables, that he may run that reades it. For the vision is yet for an apointed time, but at the end it shal speke, an not lie, tho it tarry, wait for it, because it wil surely com, twil not tarry, an no puzzle, this.

Yea also, because he transgreses by wine, he is a proud man, neeth'r keapes at home, who enlarges his desire as hel, an is as d'th, an can as not be satisfay'd, but gathers unto him awl nations, an heapes unto him awl peple.

Shal not awl these take up a parable agin him, an a taunting proverb agin him, an say, woe to him that increases that wich is not his? If one coyn be equal with one houre, then thows of the myriad coyn must for sure be the One Myriad houres in age? I trow not.

Shal they not rise up sudenly that shal bite thea, an awake that shal vex thea, an thou shalt be but booties unto them? Because thou hast spoiled many nations, awl the remnant of the peple shal spoil thea, because of the blud, an for the violence of the land, of the citi, an of awl that dwel ther'in.

Woe to him that buildes a town with blud, an doth stablise a citi by iniquity, that the peple shal labore in the very fire, that the peple shal weary themsels for ev'ry vanety.

Think on this.

They wil uterly consume awl things from of the land, man an beast. They wil consume the fowls of the heaven, an the fishes of the sea, an the stumbling blocks of the wicked. Skandalon wil cut of man from the land. Howl, ye inhabitants, for awl the peple of craft ar cut down, awl that bear silver ar cut of.

Thier guds shal becom a booty, an thier harses a desolation. For they build harses, but do not inhabit them, an they shal plant vinyards, but not drink the wine therof. I tire of this line but must many-a-time.

A day of wrath, a day of trouble an distres, a day of wastenes an desolation, a day of gloomines, of clouds an thick darknes. A day of the trumpet an alarm agin the fenced citis, an agin the high towers. I tire quickly these dayes.

And I wil bring distres pon men with mine own voice, that they shal walk like blind men, an thier blud shal be poured aht as pis, an thier flesh as the dungin. Neeth'r thier silver nor thier gold shal be able to deliver them, but the whole land shal be devowered by the fire of his jealousy, for he shal mayk ee'n a speady ridance of awl them that dwel in the land. This is the rejoicin citi that dwelt carelesly, that said in his hart, 'The Great I am, an ther is non beside me', how is he becom a desolation?

His princes within him ar roaring lions, his judges ee'ning wolves, they gnaw not the bones til' the morow. His prophets ar lite, treacherous persons. His priests hav poluted the sanctuaries. The unjust kno'es no shame, they cut of the nations, thier towers ar desolate, an mak the streats waste, that non pases by.

Let not thine 'ands be slack. Consider yewer ways. Ye hav sown much, an bring in litel. Ye eat, ye hav enuf, but ye and yewer kind ar not fil'd. Ye drink, but ye ar not fil'd with drink.

Ye clothe yur kind, but non ar warm, an he that earnes wages earnes them to put into a bag of holes. Smote with blasting, mildew an hail in awl the labores of yur hands.

Only the rich ar brok'n by tasteles desire, ded iambics an boring dinners, for them ower very names begin in the marketplayse. No more.

Thus consider yur ways. Ye looked for much, an lo, it came to litel, an wen ye brought it home, I did blow pon it, as dust. The erth is stayed from her fruit. The grisled go forth toward the north country. Soe they walked to an fro thro the erth, scat'rd with a whirlwind among awl the nations whom they knew not.

For befor these days ther was no hire for man, neeth'r was ther any peace to him that went aht or came in, because of the afliction, wich set awl men ev'ry one agin his neighboor. An a bastard shal dwel.

But they shal go with the whirlwinds of the southeast that heap up silver as shit, an fine gold as the mire of the streats. An they shal devower an subdue with sling stowns, an they shal drink, an mak a noise thro wine an be fil'd like bowls. Corn shal mayk the yung men chearful ther, an new wine the maids, an aparel, in great abundance.

But it was brok'n in that day. A burthensome stown for awl peple. Awl that burthen themsels with it shal be cut in pieces, tho awl the peple of the erth be gath'rd tog'ther agin it. Harses rifled an ravished, not joy an gladnes, an chearful feasts.

Ther'for love the truth an peace. How bonny yu ar, my awl. My love.

The burthen of the words, I hav loved yu. Wherin hast thou loved?

Yet I loved an I hayt'd an laid heritage waste. We ar impoverished, but yur eyes shal sea, an ye shal say 'be magnified', but not as that agin wich ranters rant.

If I be master, wher is my fret?

From the rising of the sun ee'n unto the going down, shal the sun of rite'ousnes arise with healing in its wings. Behold, wot a wearines it is, that wich was torn. Cursed be the deceiver.

Therfor hav I also may'd him contemptible an base befor awl the peple. Think.

Why do we deal treacherously, ev'ry man agin his broth'r, the master an the scholar, with tears, with weaping, an with crying aht. The wife of thy yuth, agin whom thou hast dealt treacherously. Yet is she not thy companion? Let non deal treacherously. Yet ye hav rob'd me. But, ye say, wherin hav we rob'd thea? In tithes an oferings.

Ye hav rob'd me, ee'n this whole nation.

Bring ye awl the tithes into the stor'arse an pour yu aht a blesin that ther shal not be room enuf to receive it.

An awl nations shal cawl yu blesed, for ye shal be a del-itesome land.

As a man that is wakened aht his sleap, deliver thyself, for Sion dwelest within Babylon.

I say agane, the trew Violation is the Violation of the self thus. An moreover we spoke of the last days, in the church of the tent mak'r.

Behold, a flying rol.

II. DUODI

i. Reconnaisance

I took a partner of hewerdom. An said unto him, let him put away his hewerdoms aht of mine site, an his adulteries, lest I strip him naked, an set him as in the day that he was born, an mayk him as a wildernes, an set him like a dry land, an slay him with thirst.

I wil go after his lovers, that give him his bred an water, wul an flax, oil an drink. Therfor, behold, I wil hedge up thy way with thewens, an mayk a wal, that he shal not find his paths. An he shal folo after his lovers, but he shal not overtake them, an he shal seke them, but shal not find them. A maze meant to lose him.

Then shal he say, I wil go an return to my husband, for then was it bet'r with me than now. For he did not kno' that I gave him corn, an wine, an oil, an multiplied his silver an gold, wich he then prepared for usurers.

Therfor wil I return, an take away my corn in the time therof, an my wine in the season therof, an wil recover my wul an my flax, given to cover his nakednes in winter.

And now wil I discover his lewdnes in the site of his lovers, an non shal deliver him aht of mine hand. I wil cause awl his mirth to cease, an I wil destroy his vines an his fig treas, wherof he hath said, these ar my rewards that my lovers hath given me. I wil mayk them a for'st, an the beasts of the field shal eat them.

He decked hisel with jewels, an he went after his lovers, an did forget me. Therfor, behold, I wil alure him, an bring him into the wildernes, into the maze an then aht, an speke comfortably unto him. An I wil give him his vinyards from thence, an a door of hope, an he shal sing ther, as in the days of his yuth, an as wen he came up aht the land.

The land hath comited great hewerdom. In the inhabitants of the land, because ther is no truth, nor mercy, nor kno'ledge. By swareing an lying an kilin an steelin, they break aht, an blud touches blud. Therfor shal the land morn, an ev'ry one that dweles ther'in shal languish. The beasts of the field, the fowls of heaven, yea, the fishes of the sea also, shal be taken away.

My peple ar destroy'd for lack of kno'ledge. Because thou hast rejected kno'ledge, I wil also reject thea, therfor wil I change thier glory into shame. They eat up the sin of my peple, an they set their hart on thier iniquity.

Awake ye drunkards an weap an howl, awl ye drinkers of wine, because of the new wine that is cut of from yewer mouth. That wich the worm hath left the locust eaten, an that wich the locust hath left the cankerworm ate, an on that the cankerworm left, spores do grow. They slide back as a backsliding heifer, thier drink is sour. In this day of ower king the princes hav may'd him sick with wine. He stretched aht his hand with scorners. The floor an the winepres shal not fead them, an the new wine shal fail. For they hav may'd ready thier hart like an oven, while they lie in wait, thier baker sleapes awl the night, in the morning it burnes as a flaming fire.

They ar hot as an oven, an hav devowered thier judges, awl thier kings ar fawlen, opresed an brok'n in judgment, because he wilingly walked. The prophet is a fule, the spiritual man is mad.

Strang'rs hav devowered his strength, an he kno'es it not. Yea, gray hairs ar here an ther pon him, yet he kno'es not, like a sily dove without hart. My love.

They hav deaply corupted themsels, they com pase a bout me with lies, with deceit. Thus judgment springeth up as hemlock in the furows of the field. Netles shal poses them. The moth'r dashed in pieces pon her children, her infants dashed in pieces, an thier women with child in turn riped up.

An I wil pour aht my wrath pon them like water. They shal tremble as a bird with the beasts of the field, an with the fowls of heaven, an with the creaping things of the ground.

ii. Delivery

Yet I wil mak them to lie down safely. I wil heal thier back-sliding, I wil love them frealy, for mine angr is turned away. I wil be as the dew.

Wot hav I to do any more with falsenes? I hav heard an observed. I am like a grean fir trea, an the just shal walk in them, but the transgresors shal fawl ther'in. I wil betroth thea unto me in rite'ousnes, an in judgment, an in loving-kindnes, an in mercies. My love. I wil ee'n betroth thea unto me in faithfulnes.

Let sin an vertue colapse. Prepare the end. Let awl be over-com an transformed in one, without contra distinction. Yu think that I play the games of the spirit? My love. An yet he gose abaht as a tale-bearer, as a vag-a-bond.

An I turned to him, ee'en eyes glazed like the miror pool of narcisus, an he spoke...

III. TRIDI

i. Trickery

In the beginning the erth was with aht form, an void. The unmoved moved pon the face of the deap. Amoeba, sead, gras, herb, fruit yielding fruit, fowl, the whale, that whose sead is in itself, an ev'ry living creature that moves, eats, fucks an kils.

He went on with this Sailor's Tale like the son of Nicoma-chus. The ape became the master of the fruit, fowl, whale an dear. Then cattle an enclosure, crop not sead, culture then cream, dominion over the fish of the sea, sead of the Kosmos, endles form. The river parted into four heds, wher ther is gold, an wher the pow'r of the river is harnesed. Wher fire is may'd, an steam an smoke, wher the lame an sick ar taken to dig a pit.

They may'd bricks instead of stown, an burned them thoroughly, for with slime they had mortar. An they built a citi an a tower, whose top reached into the sky. Fruitful multipliciti, exhausting the erth, subduing it.

They multiplied the sead as the stars of the heaven, an as the sand wich is pon the sea shore.

Now the whole erth was of one language, an of one speach, after thier families, after thier tongues, in thier lands, ee'n a'ter thier nations divided the erth, completely. They drank the wine, wer drunken an uncovered. They wer struck with blindnes, soe that they wearied to find the door.

An then she begat him, she begat her, she begat her, she begat them. An wen he awoke from his wine, he knew wot his yunger son had dun unto him. An he cursed, an may'd him a servant. An then he kiled him, he kiled her, they kiled them.

An the tricks turned aht the church do match the tricks over the sea thus. This is the time of Loki. No shapes can hold the trickster.

In such compliciti we see the brok'n midle, the mesh of adictions trew. No melodic drama, nor nete tragedy, for here is the grey without end in awl directions.

ii. Compliciti

Seke not the witeness nor the blak wen yu see the Lack thus, that we ar completed by absence. Being struck through.

Ev'rything is charged with meaning and that meaning is 'it is'. The complex'r language giv'th the lie to it, it doth not bring yu closer to it is in its full isness, its blind manifold complexity, sheer beauty and terour in one. Give up the ghost befor the ghost of a chance can return. Cease to wait and be emptied aht befor the real wait can begin. Here we may as wel end, and if yu ar sick of such tales and talk a-ready be wel gon.

Desire and such absences ar intrisickaly linked. 'His wife bore him no children in this fertile time. But they had a poor, mute maid, an soe his wife said to him, go to her, an he went, an she conseevd, an wen she saw that she had conseevd, her mistres was despised in her eyes. Wen her mistres dealt savagely with her, she fled from her face, as the gods hav fled.'

Behold, in her mouth was an olive leaf plucked of. Yay, be wel gon.

For the creature was may'd subject to vanety, not wilin'ly, but by reason of him who hath subjected the same in hope. And she said, I kno' thy works, tribulations an poverty, but thou art rich, an yet I kno' the blasphemy of them that say they ar. She that hath an ear, let her hear. Hear the things said wich hath the sharp sword with two edges. I kno' thy works, an wher thou dwelest, ee'n wher the sete of iniquity is, an thou holdest fast my name. They go to batle led by Apolo, an do batle i' the ways of Apolo. They wer like unto serpents, an had heds, for thier pow'r is in thier mouth, an with them they do hurt.

But I hav a few things agin thea. Because thou hast with yu them that cast a stumbling block befor the children. The block exists only as index, not form, tho the form of this non'tity be multiple.

Look ye not pon this as a rid'l.

Yet he shal rule them with that conundrum, as with a rod of iron, an as the vesels of a poter, shal they be brok'n to shiv'rs, ye that hath an ear. He spake his parable unto this end.

iii. Lack

And I beheld anoth'r coming up aht the erth, who exercis-
es awl the pow'r, an does great wonders, soe that he mayks
fire com down from the Kosmos on erth in site of men, saying to them that dwel on the erth, that they should mayk an
i-mage to him, an he had pow'r to give life unto the i-mage,
that the i-mage should both speke, an cause that as many
as wud not worship the i-mage to sufer. He causes awl,
both smawl an great, poor an rich, bond an frea, to receive
a mark, that no man mite buy or sel, save he that had the
mark, or the name of the beast, or the number of his name.
Here is wisdom. Let him that hath understanding count the
number of the beast, for it is the number of a man, an his
number is One Myriad. 'Tis plain that ther be men of One
Thousand Myriad, an Myriads more, Myriads without yet

names, but the mark, the mark is The One. They that hath an ear, let them hear.

And he spake further. I kno' thy works, sea thy wine an oil, look betwean an below the Ultima Thule, Crude Forties, Ekofisk, Oseberg, Bal Moral.

I kno' thy works, no more threa measures of barley for a penny, nor a measure of wheat, that thou hast a name, thou that livest, an yet art ded. No rid'l, this. The houre of temptation shal com pon awl the world, com on thea as a thief, an thou shalt not kno' wot hour.

To try them that dwel pon the erth, hold that fast wich thou hast.

I kno' thy works, that thou art neeth'r cold nor hot. Because thou art lukewarm, an neeth'r hot nor cold, I wil spew thea aht my mouth. Because thou sayest, I am rich, an increased with guds, an hav nead of nothing, an kno'est not that thou art realy wretched an miserable, poor, blind an naked. Anoint thine eyes with eyesalve, that yu mite sea. We shal be on the erth.

If any man hear my voice, an op'n the door, I wil com in to him, an wil sup with him, an he with me. He that hath an ear, let him hear.

And I say unto yu my frends. In one of the See'n Citis ther was a tower of glas, a stalagmite of sheer desiring, a rainbow round about the throw'n, in site like unto lapis lazuli of un-finite shades.

A sea of blue an green glas likened unto a crystal ful of eyes, an eyes that rest not day an night. I beheld, an I heard the voice of many round about the throw'n, an the beasts, an the elders, an the number of them was The Myriad, saying with a loud voice, worthy is the Lamb that was slain to re-ceive strength an wisdom an to give mercy. 'The cut worm forgivs the plough', yet they that hath an eye, let them not look pon this as a rid'l.

The beast has sev'ral heds. If any hath an ear, let him hear. Sion an Babylon, Alpha an Omega, the begin an end of things, he that overcoms such, shal inherit awl. Once agane, here we mite wel end, and if yu ar sick a-ready be wel gon.

They measured the wal therof, a hundred an forty an four cubits, acording to the measure of a man. It has no shrine in it, for it is a citi of man. Its midle is wide, an lo, it has no tower. Its gates ar op'n, an truly, in com sorcerers, hew-ermongers, murther'rs, idolaters an whosoev'r loves an mayks a lie.

But within ar warlocks, lovers, saviours, philosophers an thows who speke becoming truths.

This is Alpha an Omega, the beginning an ending, wot is, was, an is to com, preserved, lifted aloft, an with one stroke swiped, as a picture from its canvas. Be gon.

For the Kosmos is contradiction embodied, infinity an instance in one stroke. Agin, no rid'l this.

He continued with his tale. Spurn property, save life. Abandon wealth an seke living beings. Time an his snake that is cawled Inevitable tel us that mankind wil be destroy'd, build som'thing in wich to keap thier sead alive. Examine its foundation, inspect its kiln-fired brick with care. Soe lo, he went to the Minister of Canals for workmen. They dug an builded a shelter leagues deap. Just as dawn began to glow, he gave the workmen ale, bere an wine, as tho it wer river water, soe they could mayk a party like the New Yere. Wen awl was quiet, they gath'rd unto it.

Days paced by. Then awl that had bene blak turned to wite lite in an instant, then awl that had bene lite turned to blak'nes as fast.

The sand turned to glas, the erth to metal. The land in it shat'rd like a pot. Then it blew fast, submerging the mountain in water, overwhelming the peple. Ther fel pon men a great hail aht of heaven, ev'ry stown. Ther was a great erthquake, an the sun becom blak as the sackcloth of hair, an the moon became as blud, an the stars of heaven fel unto the erth, as a fig trea castes untimely fruits wen shaken.

No-one could see his felow, they could not re cognie each an oth'r. Awl screamed like a woman in childbirth, an they did rot inna trice. The old days had turned to clay, the deare peple fil'd the sea like soe many fish, an the sea gave up the ded in it, an life was cast into the lake of fire. Wind an flood, the storm flatening the land, pounding, the flood was a war, struggling with itself, like a madman writhing in torment. The sea calmed, fel stil, the whirlwind an flood stoped up.

The terain was flat as a roof. All was grey. An op'nd vent an fresh air fel pon the side of the faces. I fel to my kneas an sat weaping, tears streaming down, then sleap, pouring over me.

I looked around awl the day long, quiet had set in, awl of human being had turned to clay. In my bedroom D'th dwels, an wherover I set foot, ther too is Dee'th.

As surely as I shal not forget this lapis lazuli around my neck, may I be mindful of these days, an ne'r forget them, kiln-fired brick becom a sea of glas mixed with fire.

The kings of the erth, an the great men, an the rich men, an the chief captains, an the mitey men, an ev'ry bondman, an ev'ry frea man, hid themsels in the dens an in the rocks of the mountains. In the basement dede stors. They spoke to the rocks, saying 'hide us, or fawl on us.' They gnawed thier tongues for pain, an blasphemed because of thier pain, an repented not, til their own tongues wer their only feasts. The waters became wormwood, an many men died of the waters, because they wer may'd bit'r. Ther came aht the smoke, locusts pon the erth, an unto them was giv'n pow'r, as the scorpions of the erth hav pow'r. To one aroma from dee'th to d'th, to the oth'r the aroma of life to life. Who is adequate for these things?

No man was to survive the annihilation, yet thou lived the tribulation. Time an his Serpent, who kno's ev'ry machination, cared not. Soe let him wash his mat'd hair in water, cast away his rags an hav the sea cary them ther of. Let his bodi be moistened with fine oil, let the wrap around his hed be may'd anew, let him wear worthy robes an set up on his way, raising a punting pole. Yet stil he came home empty-handed. They fished deap, for things that ar hiden, for it was the way of things in thows days. They atached heavy stowns to thier feat. They dragged him down, to the ledge they puled him.

He took wot he could find, tho they pricked his hand, an he cut the heavy stowns from his feat, leting the deaps fire him. An he laid aht the things to dry, an lay down to dry hisel. A reptile silently came up an caried them of.

He sat down, weaping, his hart's blud roiled, he had not secured any gud dede. A mist went up from the erth, an watered the whole face of the ground unendingly. This caused a deap sleap to fawl, an he slept. They embalmed him.

The dove flew.

IV. QUARTIDI

i. Mediation & Counter Action

Yet the sun also aris'th, an the sun gose down, an hastes to his playse wher he arose, the unmoved moving. After just two generations the Ypocrites had decided ther wer too many. A peple becoming more an awl mitier than they. They decided to deal wisely with them, lest multipliciti overcame. They set taskmasters over them, to build treasure citis. Wen the spirit did not break, it was decread that the sons be slain, ee'n the firstborn. By the river wence it was parted, an became into four heds, they wer digging pits to put themsels in.

The river of Kishon swept him away, that ancient river, O' my soul, thou hast troden down strength. She drew him aht the water. An it came to pass in thows days that he found a trade, an aprentice of brick-making, firing them red hot, becoming master of them. The treasure citi grew quickly, but his rage was strong, blowing from the past lark the Siroco.

He brayed 'Ypocrite to dee'th with a brick, for whippin a slave. Wherfor smitest thou my felow?

The Ypocrites wer clev'r, devisers of subtl'r strategies, an thus it was may'd the fashion that ev'ry woman borow of her neighboor, to buy the exotic market spoils comon to the Ypocrites, piting neighboor agin neighboor, saying 'cadgers com and ye ar wel com.'

Chaos grip'd the world. He drifted for see'n days an nights, until he found the scene of his escape. He entered the land by night, an gathr'd wot was left of his peple by the pits. He broke thier work with a flame of fire aht the midst of a cruse of oil.

He spoke to them like thunder. They broke nor sowen, an shal strike.

He went up the hil to speke with the Ypocrites. He said, who may'd thea a prince an judge over us? Pon thy cattle wich is i' the field, pon the horses, pon the ases, pon the oxen an pon the sheap, ther shal be a very grievous murain.

An soe they came to pass ther in victory.

ii. Departure

But while he was away, his peple began to worship the golden cups. They broke strike an he roared at them, an the peple scat'rd thro' an aht the nations o' the erth. Go up to London, that great citi, write write write. To the tribes who ar dispers'd abroad, on various trials. To mak a diference betwean the unclene an the clene, betwean the beast that may be eaten an the beast that may not. On purity an clenelines, on performing an incense ofering at an unprescribed time, on wot is rite an gud to eat an wotnot. On birth, on skin disease, fungus, mildew, genital discharge, particularly female, with penalties imposed for unlaweful observance, the worship of mediums, witches, parental irev'rence, unlaweful mariage, sex an unacseptable bodily defects. Blasphemers die.

The Ypocrites wer too many, he wrote a treatise over two hundred pages in length. Thee'n wer becoming more an mitier each day. Multipliciti was overcoming.

He won ofice in the local consul, set taskmasters over the Ypocrites, to build pits, mayk bricks, firing them red hot, borowing of thier neighboors, worshiping the golden cups.

He wrote 'and awl is wel in the land, an the children of the land who ar scat'rd ar wel instructed.'

He put aht a cawl for the scat'rd peples to be counted, an lo, thier number was great. He wished for thier return an sent aht mesengers begging. But the sceptics floeer'd among the scat'rd tribes, spredding myths mong thier camps. 'It is floeing with pis an shit' they said, an the tribes refused to re-enter the land. He went up to a bald spot, to a bar'n height. He screamed an declaimed, that the scat'rd ones destroy'd thier idols.

A plague broke aht, caried by fleas from rats. Wooden water troughs wer blamed an drained, then razed. Then came the great thirsting. The Ypocrites wer thus leveled. He comanded water aht a rock. Non came.

He ordered a masacre of the remaining Neocrites, saying 'ev'ry man wil be armed for war, to do batle an yu wil destroy awl this peple.'

A river of blud non can drink ran thro the square.

By the stown benches built for the old to sit in the sun, by the marble pilars modeled on the treas of the ancient templ clereings, bodies an a cloud of locusts ten miles acros. Yea, awl hav transgresed thy law, ee'n by departing.

Let us build us a citi an a tower, whose top may reach up, build armies an dogs trained for the ravishing. They renamed the citis, an the sites of murther. The Lawes wer thus drawn in tablets of stown an set into the wals of the templ, that the avenger must kil the murther'r wen he metes him. But if he strikes him aht of hatred an he dies, the one who struck him must surely be put to d'th, for he is a murther'r.

The comun-ity must judge betwean the slayer an the avenger of blud, an deliver the slayer aht of thier hand to the avenger of blud, to be kiled.

Thier decision wil be presided over by a High Priest, an these things must be a statutory ordinance for yu thro'out yewer generations, in awl the playses wher yu live.

For the first law had bene giv'n that 'thou shalt not'. But stil they strayed, an a second law, a Deuteronomium, of fresh complexity, was required. It ran:

'Thou shalt not. Thou shalt not. Thou shalt not. Thou shalt not. Thou shalt not. Thou shalt not. Thou shalt not. Thou shalt not. Thou shalt not. Thou shalt not.'

Violation to the violator, ofense to the ofender. An his sons embalmed him an playsed him in a cofin. He is ded, now therfor arise, go, an awl this peple, unto the land to be giv'n to them. Ther shal not any man be able to stand befor thea awl the days of thy life, as I was with Him, soe I wil be with thea.

I wil not fail thea, nor forsake thea.

Be strong an of gud courage, for unto this peple thou shal divide for an inheritance the land, wich I sware unto thier fath'rs to give them, that thou mayest observe to do awl acording to awl of The Lawe, wich my servant comanded thea, turn not from it to the rite hand or to the left, that thou mayest prosper whithersoev'r thou goest.

This book of The Lawe shal not depart aht thy mouth, but thou shalt meditate ther'in day an night, that thou mayest observe to do acording to awl that is writen ther'in, for then thou shalt mak thy way prosperous, an then thou shalt hav gud suces, an' c'n'c.

Yur wives, yur litel ones, catle, land, laws, land.

Ye shal pass befor yur br'thren armed, an poses the land. Then ye shal return unto the land of yur posesion, an enjoy it. That wich He gave yu toward the sunrisin.

Whosoev'r rebel agin thy comandment, an wil not hearken unto thy words, he shal be put to d'th, an ye shal be watched thus, only be strong an of gud courage.

Behold now I hav op'nd my mouth, my tongue hath spoken in my mouth. If thou canst answer me, set thy words in order befor me, stand up. Such is the price of the leavings.

iii. The Altruist

And yet one arose an spoke back to answer the venturer. He was named by fame The Altruist. That prisons ar built with stowns of law, brothels with bricks of religion. That the ancient poets animated awl sensible objects with geniuses. They gave them names an adorned them with the properties of woods, rivers, mountains, lakes, citis, nations, an whaytv'r thier enlarg'd an numerous senses could percieve.

They studied the genius of ev'ry citi an country, placing it under its mental deity, 'til a system was formed, wich some took advantage of, an enslaved the vulgar, by atempting to realise or abstract the mental deities from thier objects. Thus began Priesthood. Choosing forms of worship from poetical tales.

And at length they pronounced that the Gods had giv'n this, had ordered such things. Thus men forgot that awl deities reside only in the human brest. My senses discovered the unfinite in ev'rything. The poetic genius, as yu now cawl it, was the first principle, an awl oth'rs merely derivative, wich was the cause of ower despising the priests an philosophers of oth'r countries, an of ower prophecying. The Greak poets sang the citis into being, above architects an Kings. It is the tributaries of the poetic genius that the King desires soe fervently, an invokes soe patheticaly, saying that by this he conquers an governs.

An we soe love ower ways that we curse in his name awl deities of surounding nations, an asert that they hav rebeled.

Our ways ar sinful as such, how should we raise ower eyes? Ower voices hath used deceit. How should I cawl on truth? The damps of d'th fawl thick pon me, horours gawp me in the face. I look behind, ther is no returning from the gawping, d'th folo's after me. I walk in regions of d'th, wher no trea is, without a lantern to direct my steps, without a stave to suport me. The curtains of darknes wer drawn. I am wraped in mortality. My flesh is a prison, my bones the bars of d'th.

Yet voices of comfort ar heard over the carch of d'th, an thy yuth breathes aht its soul with joy into eternity.

Misery builds over ower roofs, an discontent hath burst its banks. Yet wher the cold clay breathed with life, an ower ancestors, who now sleap in thier graves, on these plains, an in these silent woods, trew joys descend. Here build thy nest, fix thy staf, delites blosom around.

Numberles beauties spring in the nimble air, the brook stretches its silver inhabitants, the sky glit'rs jingling. The whole creation wil apear unfinite, wheras it now apears finite an corupt. This wil com to pass by an improvement of sensual enjoyment. But first, the notion that man has a bodi distinct from his soul, is to be expunged, this I shal do by printing in the infernal m'thod, by corosives, wich in Hel ar salutary an medicinal.

They melt aparent surfaces away, an display the unfinite wich was hid. If the doors of perception wer clenesed ev'rything wud apear to man as it is, unfinite, for man has caged hisel up, until he seas awl things thro narow slits. As unity is the cloak of foly, soe gudnes is the cloak of knavery. Thows who wil hav unity exclusively, or find it in but one playse, com aht with a moral like a sting in the tail.

But think not thro the gud as the countryside. My words ar to the citi alike. The son of Nicomachus says characters ar eeth'r gud or bad. Now gudnes or badnes has nothing to do with character, a gud window or a bad is a window stil. A horse is not more a lion for being a bad horse. Unity an morality ar secondary considerations, an belong to exception an not to rule, to acident an not to substance. Awl is so, an Ego thus, not more or less ego, but ego for the gud an the bad, it doth fluctuate in one man, moment to moment.

The Anciéns caled it eating of the trea of gud an evil. Gud an evil ar riches an poverty, a trea of misery propagating generation an d'th. Ev'ry poem must necesarily be a perfect unity, but why Homer's is peculiarly soe I canot tel. But wen a work has unity, it is as much in a part as in the whole. The torso is as much a unity as the bodi.

An yet the Ratio an the Relative hav lately conspired, an dun much evil. Conjecture as 'thic becom Rule, cast as a mistery over the real law of the Ratio. The whole as hole.

It is these that now desolate with wars. Wot can be created can be destroy'd.

Yu must leve fath'rs an moth'rs an harses an lands if they stand in the way of this art.

Money is the great monster of reason, the root of gud an evil, in this acusation of sin.

Without unceasing practice nothing can be dun. If yu leve of such yu ar lost. I say furthermore, grievous corection lies in wait for him that forsakes his own, strange, dificult path, of myriad complexity. Man has no notion of moral fitnes but from education. He is only a natural organ subject to sense, who ca'not perceive but thro his bodily organs. Man by his reasoning pow'r can only compare an judge of wot he has already perceived, an' c'n'c.

From a perception of only threa senses or threa elements, non could deduce a fourth or fifth.

Non could hav oth'r than natural or organic thots, if he had non but organic perceptions. Man's desires ar limited by his perceptions, non can desire wot he has not perceived. The desires an perceptions of man, untaught by owt but organs of sense, must be limited to objects of sense.

And yet man's perceptions ar not bound by organs of perception, he perceives more than sense, tho often soe acute, can discover. Reason, or the Ratio, of awl we hav already know'n, is not the same that it shal be wen we kno' more. Wot is now proved was once only imagined.

Man mayks instruments an with the lathe oth'r machines. These ar augmented to man, to enlarge his perceptions an sea into anoth'r age, wich demands augmentation as yet unsene. The bounded is loathed by its posesor. The same circulur, ee'n of the universe, wud sune becom a mil with complicated wheals.

An thus, we labore within.

Yet 'more' is the cry of a mistaken soul, les than awl ca'not satisfy man.

If any could desire wot he is incapable of posesing, despair must be his eternal lot. Agane, grievous corection lies for him that forsakes his own path. The desire of man being unfinite, the posesion is unfinite. If it wer not for the poetic or prophetic character, the philosophic an experimental wud sune be at the ratio of awl things, an stand stil, unable to do oth'r than repeat the same dul round over an agane.

An soe it is in this day. He who seas the unfinite in awl things seas infinity. He who seas the ratio seas hisel only.

And yet I conjecture that the poetic, prophetic an the ratio do combine to great evil as wel as gud. Art is the trea of life. Science is the trea of d'th. For ev'ry pleasure money is useles. How is it that thou ca'not eat gold an yet stil fead thy children with such?

An no rid'l, this.

The unfinite is art an not money. Money is its curse. Art degraded, imagination denied, war governs the nations. The unproductive man is not the destroyer. Ther ar states in wich awl visionary men ar acounted mad men.

Awl that we sea is vision, from generated organs, gon as sune as com, permanent in the imagination, considered as nothing by the natural man. Nature has no ahtline, but imagination has, ther is no tune but imagination. Nature has no supranature, an doth disolve.

Imagination is eternity an eternity is imagination. It is awl a vane delusion of the al-creative imagination. The cunning sures an the aim-at-thines do deny, an the pickthanks an blockeads. I hav bene caled a madman, yet a fule they cawl thea.

I wonder wich they envy the more? They nev'r flinch, but keap up thier lip, about liberty, an Jenny suck awa'.

If yu mean to please ev'rybodi, yu wil set to work both ignorance an skil. For a great multitewd ar ignorant, an skil to them seams as raving an rant. Like puting oil an water in a lamp, they mak a great smoke an a sputer. Ther is no use of liteing a lamp wen yu don't wish to sea. The vanities ar the same.

The great philosophers sat tog'ther thinking of nothing but thier greatnes, an how they may increase, endeavouring to conceal laughter or hayt thus. Wher any view of money exists - tha' evil abstract - art ca'not be caried on, but war only, by pretence to the two imposibilities, chastity an abstinence, the gods of the hethen. Heroism is a miser.

Eat dung if thou neadst an lay long on yewer left side, for the desire of raising oth'r men into a perception of the unfinite. Is he honest who resists his genius or conscience only for the sake of present ease or gratification? Nay. Tho certain sounds do liteen the weight of the world, some lift it completely, if only briefly. Wot became smoke was in us, as we met each fortnight, nev'r fuly reconciled with the unfinite, or one an' oth'r. Oposition is trew frendship. Salt poured on hope as some left, yet stil wer as one, with ower sword arms frea.

No sword sleaps from unceasing mental fite. Drive yewer cart an plow over the bones of the ded.

The road of exces leads to the palayce of wisdom. Prudence is a rich ugly old maid courted by incapaciti. He who desires but acts not, breads pestilence.

Awl sacred codes hav bene the cause of the eror that man has two principles, of bodi an soul. That the energy cal'd evil is alone from the bodi an that reason, cal'd gud, is alone from the soul. I say nay. Infinity wil torment man in eternity as he folo's his energies.

But the folowing contraries to these things ar trew, that man has no bodi distinct from his soul, for that cal'd bodi is a portion of soul discern'd by the five senses, the chief inlets of soul in the earlier age.

Energy is the only life an from the bodi an reason is the bound or ahtward circumference of energy. 'Energy is eternal delite', it has bene said. Thows who restrain desire do soe because thiers is weak enuf to be restrained, an the restrainer of reason usurps its playse an governs the unwiling. An being restrain'd, it by degreas becoms pasive, 'til it is only the shadow of desire. Sune'r deeth than nurse unacted desires. Dip him in the river who loves water.

A fule seas not the same trea that a wise man seas. Eternity is in love with the productions of time, as Chronos with his snake sister Ananke. The bea has no time for sorow, but neeth'r doth it labore, nor the plants of the field, they toil not, neeth'r do they swett. The hours of foly ar measured by the clock, but of wisdom no clock can measure.

Awl wholsome food is caught without net or trap. Bring aht number, weight an measure, but only in a year of derth. No bird soars too high, if he soars with his own wings. A ded bodi ree'nges not injuries.

V. QUINTIDI

i. Reaction

And yet they did dare to reply The Altruist further. Swareing an damning as acts ar nothing distinct from the act of prayer an praises. Why dost thou wonder? Why art thou angry? They ar awl one in themsels, no more purity in one than the oth'r.

Expres, Hermes, a mesenger com from among them, in a state of confusion, 'they do not sea the sky that crowns them.' Is ther only sky above? Flat, smooth, deap, without edges or landmarks. Within ower consecrated forms of expresion, therfor, this an that stand ireconcilably oposed, but flatened for the mases only into the diference betwean The One an The Many.

The lineaments of the wider asemblage of the ev'ryday ar obscured, as ower mind lives, aht of shear necesity, on this easy plane. Here ar talking hieroglyphs, about wich it is imposible to be mistaken, wher 'meaning' is hapily drowned. We can only sea nothing via the 'oth'r' of som'thing, an then on into sensation, quantity, quality.

The Altruist took see'n breaths befor braking silence.

'Thine own mouth condemnes thea, an not I, thine own lips testify agin thea, if at awl they do.

I weigh not how I am judged, in that I judge not my self. The censures of kin, of the mitey, ar no more to me than a swating at a fly. Dialectic not Deuteronomy. Dost thou think a Triteronemy and more like as to bea more than the swating of the fly to me? Quadronomy, Quintonomy. Awl thows acts arising from the pow'r ar as pure as the pow'r. Thier names ar mere veils an the like. Sin hath its conception only in the imagination, that this act is gud, or that act is evil. Its origin doth spring from such webs.'

He sigh'd.

'Yea, that wich by yu is imagined evil, anoth'r of the same substance imagines gud. David did use his pow'r to take Bathsheba, an stil yet her purity is most oft spoken as a question? Yet more speke of her shame. Enuf.'

Thus they responded with gladness giv'n to The Altruist, having passed the test by failing.

ii. The Magical Object

He broke silence agin. Mistery, Kosmos, vast infinity. Wot shal I say thou art? Wen thou canst be named? Wot shal I speke of thea, wen in spekeing of 'thea' I speke nothing but contradiction? For if I say I sea thea, it is nothing but the seaing of thyself, for ther is nothing in me capable of seaing owt but thyself. I sea with yur eyes. If I say I kno' thea, that is no oth'r than kno'ledge o' thyself.

For I am of thea. If I say I love thea, it is nothing so, my sekeing of thea is non oth'r than the sekeing of mine self. My delite in thea is non oth'r than delite in myself, in inconceivable ways.

As awl things wer let aht of thea, soe they shal give up their Being, life, hapines, misery, into thea agane. Tho the clothing disolve an com to nothing, thea liv'th on, an I, tis clere, live in thea, Kosmos, ee'n after.

One single uncompounded an unseparated glory, in whose intrinsical womb variety lies ocult, 'til time orderly brings it forth.

I lie quietly secure in the silence of infinity, at this crossing in many roads. While I sea the whole world consumed in the fire of envy, one agin the oth'r. I hear much noise about me, but it serves only to deafen me, an on into the stil slumbers of the unfinite. The formal world is much afriteed, ev'ry form is up in arms to proclaim op'n wars pon itself. Dashing one thing agin the oth'r, that wich he formerly faced with the glory of his own presence, he set'th up an castes down, an who shal say 'wot doest thou?'

While we perambulate in variety, we walk but as soe many shadows or ghosts in it, that itself being but the umbrage of unity. To descend from the onenes or eternity, into the multipliciti, is to lose ourself in the endles labyrinth. To then ascend from variety to unity, wud be to find ourself as we wer befor we wer.

But how shal a man atain a onenes? Seaing ther is no way probable for us, we must patiently expect its seasonal descension 'pon us. Whose name it is to consume us unto itself, melt us into the same nature an likenes.

An truly, until this coms to manifest, awl that man does to acquire ful satisfaction does multiply sorow on his hed an augment cares on his spirit. Dark is the path of oth'rs, for the one that fled his own.

I sometimes hear from the world, wich I hav now forsaken. I sea its diurnals ar fraught with the tidings of the same clamour an strife wich abounded wen I left it. An mine own past presents clues, shraps on the waves to be plucked an read. I give it the hearing, an that is awl.

Felow creatures, awl brought into this world without propriety, Mine an Thine, no such title as theft with wich it may be damned. For the pree'ntion hereof they did take the comons, soe that awl mite live of themsels. No nead of defrauding, but unity with one anoth'r.

This I conscevd because I knew not wot I was befor I came into being. The spirit of man while in the bodi is distinct from infinity. The bodi is thus may'd distinct, seperated an automated, perambulatory, peripateticaly, but forver after shal kno' nothing, after this, my Being, disolves.

But as a stream from the ocean was distinct in itself, while it was a stream, but then returned to the ocean an was not one with it, without distinction, but was gon entirely in it, without trace. An yet... tis the trace that is the whole working. Vast condensations of traces, mist on the glass halts seaing, to produce only seeing...

Mak distinctions thus, the pow'r distinct from The Power, being from Being an seeing from seaing.

Reduce gud an evil to dust for both ar servants to me.

An yet my wish for thier doom iluminates them as unruly forces within, nay, my wish is of such force. Of that wich is said to live in perfect majesty, fie then, for shame, look not above the skies, lest ye look for rocks.

Look in, but then aht, to yur felow creature. Sin hath its conception deap buried in the imagination, therfor soe long as the act was in infinity, or nakedly produced by infinity, it was as of the unfinite.

But afterward ther is an apearance in thea, or aprehension of thea, that this act is gud, or that act is evil. An it has bene said trew many a time without ev'r bein in eror, that the 'thic is unexpresably complicated. To some more clerely, to some more obscurely, kno' that sin is in yu.

Felow creature, awl is ours an awl is wel. Ther is no king but the Kosmos. A single eye, awl lite, no darknes, or lite an darknes one, universality revealed. I came not into the world to condemn, but to save. 'D'th wher is thy sting? Grave, thy victory?'

The whole creation, awl is one most swete an lovely, my love, my bonny. I an i. Therfor consider, that without act, no life, without mortal life, no infinity, an without mortality, no eternal peace an freadom, in dede, in pow'r, wich is infinity, ruling an damning awl into itself without end, forver.

Yet notwithstanding awl of this, I hav a relenting lite in me, freting awl this mite not be so, as oth'rs do say, an most violently. But howev'r, a cup of wine should wash away this doubt.

iii. Guidance

But this sermon from within ended, it was writ plain in noise above that no thing was solved without. And soe he continued with his longer tale, at the church of the tent mak'r, as the blasting continued without.

Of how he sent aht two men to spy secretly, saying, go view the land, within an without. An they went, an came into her harse of unrepute, an lodged ther. An they wer sought aht. But she brought them up to the roof of the harse, an hid them with the stalks of flax, wich she had laid in order pon the roof. An the men pursued after them the way, an after they wer gon aht, shut the gate.

And she said unto the men, I kno' that yur teror is fawlen pon us, an that awl the inhabitants of the land faint because of yu, but neeth'r did ther remain any more courage in any man because of yu. Now therfor, I pray yu, sware unto me that ye wil save alive my fath'r, an my moth'r, an my br'thren, an my sisters, an awl that they hav, an deliver ower lives from d'th. An the men ansr'd her, ower life for thine, if ye uter not this ower busines.

An it shal be, wen we hav the land, that we wil deal kindly an truly with thea.

Then she let them down by a cord thro the window, for the harse of unrepute was pon the town wal. An she said unto them, get yu to the mountain, lest the pursuers meat yu, an hide yurselves ther threa days, until the pursuers be returned, an afterwards may ye go yewer way. An the men said unto her, we wil be blameles of this thine oath wich thou hast may'd us sware.

Behold, wen we com into the land, thou shalt bind this line of scarlet thread in the window wich thou didst let us down by, an thou shalt bring thy fath'r, an thy moth'r, an thy br'thren, an awl thy fath'r's harsehold, home unto thea.

An it shal be, that whosoev'r shal go aht of the doors of thy harse into the streat, his blud shal be pon his hed, an we wil be giltles, an whosoev'r shal be withtheain the harse, his blud shal be on ower hed, if any hand be pon 'im. An if thou uter this ower busines, then we wil be quit of thine oath wich thou hast may'd us sware.

And she said soe be it, an sent them away, an they departed, an she bound the scarlet line i' the window. An they went, an came unto the mountain, an abode ther threa days, until the pursuers wer returned, an the pursuers sought them thro aht awl the way, but found them not.

So the two men returned, an descended from the mountain, an paced over, an told awl things that befel them, an they said, awl the inhabitants of the country do faint because of us. An they comanded the peple, saying, 'wen ye sea the traveling Library of The Lawe, then ye shal remove from yur playse, an go after it.'

Yet ther shal be a spayce betwean yu an it, com not nere unto it, that ye may kno' the way by wich ye must go, for ye hav not paced this way heretofor. An he said, Hereby ye shal kno' that we wil without fail drive aht awl from befor yu.

The Library of The Lawe pases befor yu.

Now take ye twelve men aht of ev'ry tribe a man, the waters shal be cut of, an they shal stand pon a heap. An it came to pas, wen the peple removed from thier tents, to pass over, an Folow The Lawe. An they had paced over into the new land, an they did feast, an may'd sharp knives, an circumcised the children at the hil of the forskins. Awl the men of war died in the wildernes by the way. Now awl that wer born in the wildernes thows forty yeares, they had not circumcised. An thus wer they marked aht, no shibbol'th of bodi or mouth. Oftentimes no marking is a mark, an no rid'l, this.

The citi was straitly shut up, non went aht, an non came in.

Take the Library of The Lawe an the great noisemak'rs an mak noise until the wal of the citi fawls down flat, an the peple shal ascend up, let him that is armed pass on befor the Library of The Lawe.

And it came to pas. An the citi shal be acursed, ee'n it, an awl that ar ther'in, only she shal live, an awl that ar with her in the harse, because the mesengers that we sent wer hid.

But awl the silver, an gold, an vesels of brass an iron, ar con-secrated, they shal com into the treasury of the Library of The Lawe, wich contanees The Ban, that yu shal not sufer The Oth'r to live.

And they uterly destroy'd awl that was in the citi, both man an woman, yung an old, an ox, an sheap, an as with the edge of the sword. But He had said unto the two men that had spied aht the country, 'go into her harse, an bring aht thence, an awl that she hath, as ye swore.' An the yung men that wer spies went in, an brought her an kin aht, an awl ther'in. An they burnt the citi with fire, an awl that was ther'in, only the silver an the gold, an the vesels of bras an iron, they put into the treasury of the Library of The Lawe. This fame was noised thro' aht awl the country.

But they comited a trespas in the acursed thing. They did not do acording to awl of The Lawe. They turned from it, to the rite hand an to the left. Lo, then went up thither about threa thousand men, an smote thirty an six great men, for they chased them from befor the gate an smote them in the going down, wherfor the harts of the peple melted, an became as a thewin water. An lo, she wept, an he rent his clothes, an fel to the erth pon his face befor the Library of The Lawe until ee'ntide, he an the elders, an put shit pon thier heds. An thus the land was Divided by Lot. In Lot Twenty-Six ther was a weaping an a wailing, an Lot Forty-Nine a great confusion, as in the Vileins of Lot Hundred, on the edge.

An he spake thus, that the One was over the one short of the hundred, an yet a false equation ca'not hold the Hundreds, an no rid'l this. Let my words be marked.

An yet stil she wept. The land had rest forty yeares, befor the peple strayed from The Lawe once more. Yet ye hav not obeyed, why hav ye dun this? I wil not drive thine enemies aht from befor yu, but they shal be as thorns in yewer sides, an thier ways shal be a snare unto yu.

Think on.

The peple lifted up thier voice, an wept, an ther arose anoth'r generation after them, wich knew not, an wer too delivered into the hands of spoilers that spoiled them, an sold into the hands of thier enemies round about, soe that they could not any longer stand befor thier enemies, nor kno' it.

One took the dagger from his rite thigh, an thrust it into his bely, an the haft also went in after the blade, an the fat closed pon the blade, soe that he could not draw the dagger aht of his bely, an the dirt came aht. An he said unto her, give me, I pray thea, a litel water to drink, for I am thirsty. An she op'nd a botle of milk, an gave him drink, an covered him. Then his wife took a nail of the tent, an took a hamer in her hand, an went softly unto him, an smote the nail into his templs, an fastened it into the ground, for he was fast asleap an weary. Soe he died.

Anoth'r came. He asked water, an she gave him milk, she brought forth buter in a lordly dish. She put her hand to the nail, an her rite hand to the workman's hamer, an with the hamer she smote away his hed, wen she had pierced an stricken thro his templs.

He fel, wher he bowed, ther he fel down ded.

A deliverer was raised up yet once more, who delivered them from thier own doing. Hav they not sped? Hav they not divided the prey? To ev'ry man a damsel or two, a prey of diverse cul'r?

The peple met as one man for the necks of them that take the spoil. Soe let awl thine enemies perish. An the land had rest anoth'r forty yeares. But they did evil, an wer delivered once more into the hands of evil. An the land had rest forty yeares. An agane they did evil, an wer delivered agane into the hand of evil. An the land.

He saw her. One of the dawters of the Ypocrites. Fine hair on her lip. He bade her swipe it from her face, but she protested, for this was her pow'r. Then he came up an told her fath'r an moth'r, now get her me as my wife, but shav her. An it was dun. Neighboors gath'rd tog'ther as befor a new woman. Behold, here is my dawter, a maiden, an his concubine, that I wil bring aht now, an he brought her forth unto them, an they knew her, an abused her awl the night until the morning, an wen the day began to spring, they let her go.

Then came the woman in the dawning of the day, an fel down at the door of the harse wher he was. An he rose up in the morning, an op'nd the doors of the harse, an went aht to go his way, an behold, the woman, his concubine, was fawlen down at the door of the harse, an her hands wer pon the threshold.

And he said unto her, up, an let us be going. But no answer. Then the man took her bodi up. An wen he was com into his harse, he took a knife, an laid hold on his concubine, an divided her bodi, tog'ther with her bones, into twelve pieces, an sent her to the twelve coasts of the island. An it was so, that awl that saw it said ther was no such dede dun nor sene from the day.

Consider of it, take advice an speke yur minds, I took my concubine, an cut her in pieces, an sent her thro'aht awl the country, for they hav comited lewdnes an foly.

And awl the peple arose as one man, saying, we wil go up by Lot agin it. Soe awl the men wer gath'rd agin the citi, knit tog'ther as one man. They wer him. But wot wickednes is this that is dun among yu?

In thows days ther was no king, ev'ry man did that wich was rite in his own eyes. Stalked becom stalker, abused abuser.

Her sister was suposed to be the ancestor of Him, the great one, but they only had her saying-so, an many caled her bred unwholesome. But we took her saying so, the family hath becom as the mez of the unswept threshing floor, an thus we wiled ourselves blind. An they read from the Oth'r Book, that wich had not bene read, saying 'yu shalt not give yur dawters to thier sons, or take thier dawters for yur sons or for yurselves.'

And Sister was sent for. 'Behold, he winnowes barley tonight in the threshing floor. Wash thyself therfor, an anoint thea, an put thy raiment pon thea, an get thea down to the floor.

Wen he lies down, thou shalt mark the playse wher he shal lie, an thou shalt go in, an uncover his feat, an laytheedown.

He wil tel thea wot thou shalt do.'

And she said 'al that thou sayest unto me I wil do.' An she went down unto the floor, an did acording to awl. An wen he had eaten an drunk, an his hart was mery, he went to lie down at the end of the heap of corn, an she came softly, an uncovered his feat, an laid her down. An he said, Blesed be thou of Him, my dawter, for thou hast showed more kindnes in the later end than at the beginning, inasmuch as thou folo'edst not yung men, wh'ther poor or rich. An now, my dawter, fret not, I wil do to thea awl that thou requirest, for awl the citi of my peple doth kno' that thou art a virtuous woman.

And now it is trew, she said, that I am thy nere kinsman, howbeit ther is a kinsman nereer than I? But he said let it not be kno'n that a woman came into the floor. Also he said, Bring the veil that thou hast pon thea, an hold it. I shal sele a parcel of land, wich was ower broth'rs. An it was bought for her, an thus the line went on, from without, within, an within without. A prey of divers'r cul'r.

VI. SEXTIDI

i. Strife

Thus land begat land. Coyn begat coyn. He may'd a gret throw'n of ivory, an overlaid it with the best gold. The throw'n had sev'n steps, an the top of the throw'n was round. Ther wer stays on eeth'r side of the playse of the sete, an two lions stood beside the stays. An twelve lions stood ther on the one side an on the oth'r pon the see'n steps.

Ther was not the like may'd in any oth'r time of this spirit. An awl his drinking vesels wer of gold, an awl the vesels of the harse wer of pure gold, non wer of silver. It was nothing acounted of in his days. He had at sea a navy, bringing ivory, apes an peacocks.

He loved many strange women. He was a person whose eratic fortune had caried an shewn him many forin zones, an of no obscure family. One, two or threa an forty yeares of age. Indif'rent, blondhair'd an of an ominus, pensive, melancholic aspect. Of a pestilent an prevalent logical discourse in most company, not giv'n much to talk, or to mayk suden reply, of a most imperious an dang'rous hiden pride of hart, despising the wisest of neighboors for thier ignorance, most ambitious an arogant.

He exceaded awl for riches an for wisdom, an awl the erth sought to hear his wisdom, an they brought vesels of silver, an vesels of gold, an garments, a rate year by year, an linen yarn at a price.

Strange news is com from abroad, od tales ar caried, tis in the wind. Yewer iniquities hav separated yu an the unkno'n, an yur sins hav hid thier face from yu. For yewer hands ar defil'd with blud, an yewer fingers with the iniquity of thows who do yer abidin.

Yur lips ave spoken lies, yur tongue hath muted perversnes.

Non cal's for justice, nor any pleade for truth, they trust in vanety, an speke lies. They conseev mischief, an bring forth iniquity. They weve the spider's web. Thier webs shal not becom garments, neeth'r shal they cover themsels with their works. Thier works ar works of iniquity, an the act of violence is in thier hands.

ii. Branding

Thier feat run to evil, an they mak haste to shed innocent blud, thier thots ar thots of iniquity. Wasting an destruction ar in thier paths. The Book of Jasher burns.

The way of peace they kno' not, an ther is no judgment in their goings, they hav may'd them crooked paths. Whosoev'r gose ther'in shal not kno' peace. Therfor is judgment far from us, neeth'r doth justice overtake us. We wait for lite, but behold obscurity, look for britenes, but we walk in darknes.

We grope for the wal like the blind, an we grope as if we had no eyes, we stumbl at noon day as in the night, we ar in desolate playses as ded men. We roar like bears an morn sore like doves, we look for judgment, but ther is non, for salvation, but it is far of from us, for truth is fawlen in the streat, an equity ca'not enter.

Vexations of the tongue for the keaping on...

... Let me ...

My son, in his gate ...

Bit'rly yu ...

Yu hold ...

... in his gate ...

At one double houre ...

the darknes was dense ...

it did not alow him to sea.

In his face the Bul spat slaver,

with the tuft of its tail ...

As they say the knife ...

At two double hours ...

the darknes was dense ...

it did not alow him to sea.

... skilfuly worked,

... he provided for his friend.

... he provided for his friend,

... betwean them, mounted ...

At threa double hours ...

the darknes was dense ...

it did not alow him to sea.

... was thier ...

... was thier thicknes,

... was thier ... he provided for his friend,

... he provided for his friend.

At four double hours ...

the darknes was dense ...

it did not alow him to sea.

... a chair of lapis lazuli ...

... a staf of lapis lazuli ...

... that exists I kno' inded.

Why do yu desire to do this thing?

... owt ... do yu want soe much?

At five double hours ...

the darknes was dense ...

it did not alow him to sea.

... the scapegoat ... of the teaming n'therworld ...

...wich we ...

... thier ... thier names ...

... judge of ...

On reaching six double hours

the darknes was dense ...

it did not alow him to sea.

... he conseevd of daming the river ...

... already I stord,

... already I grew.

At see'n double hours ...

the darknes was dense ...

it did not alow him to sea.

thro sorow ...

by frost an by sunshine my face is burnt ...

thro exhaustion ...

now yu ...

At eight double hours he was hurying ...

At nine double hours the north wind ...

One reaching ten double hours ...

... was very nere ...

Ther was briliance ... the treas ...

... she lifted her hed,

in order to watch him ...

Elee'n double hours ... the deluge ...

the darknes was dense ...

... Let me ...

... Ypocrites ... becom Neocrites ...

Supose a woman has ... an loses ... lite a lamp ...

Sweap the harse an search, carefuly, until she finds it?

Further references, sources and inspirations

Agamben (1998) *Homo Sacer: Sovereign Power and Bare Life*. Stanford University Press.

Agamben (2006) *The Time That Remains*. Stanford University Press.

Agamben (2011) *The Highest Poverty*. Stanford University Press.

Alexander (trans., 1996 [900+]) *The Earliest Poems in English*. Harmondsworth: Penguin.

Arendt, Hannah (1999 [1968]) Introduction to *Illuminations*. London: Pimlico.

Aristotle (1987 [-350]) *De Anima*. Harmondsworth: Penguin.

Augustine (1961 [400]) *Confessions*. London: Penguin.

Augustine (2003 [426]) *City of God*. London: Penguin.

Benjamin, Walter (2006 [1938]) 'Theopolitical Fragment' in *Selected Writings* Vol. 3: 1935-1938. Harvard.

Benjamin, Walter ([1940]) *Theses On History*, translated by Harry Zorn, in Illuminations. London: Pimlico.

Benjamin, Walter (2005 [1940]) *Theses On History* translated by Dennis Redmond.

Britt, Brian (2010) 'The Schmittian Messiah in Agamben's The Time That Remains' in *Critical Inquiry*, Vol. 36, No. 2. University of Chicago Press. pp. 262-287.

Bible, The (2008 [1611]) the Oxford 'authorised' *King James with Apocrypha*. Oxford: OUP.

Blake (2002) *Collected Poems*. London: Routledge.

Brower Latz, Andrew (2015) 'Gillian Rose and Social Theory' in *Telos* No.173 Gillian Rose special issue. Winter 2015.

Chare, Nicholas (2011) *Auschwitz and Afterimages: Abjection, Witnessing and Representation*. London: I.B. Tauris.

Chvatik, Ivan (2006) 'Jan Patocka and his "Care for the Soul" in the "Post-European" World'. *Center for Theoretical Study and Jan Patocka Archive.*

George (trans., 2003) *Gilgamesh*. London: Penguin.

Hegel (1976 [1807]) *The Phenomenology of Spirit*. USA: Galaxy.

Hegel (2015 [1812]) *The Science of Logic*. Cambridge University Press.

Hegel, in (ed., Houlgate, 1996) *The Hegel Reader*. Oxford: Blackwell.

Hill, Christopher (1991) *The World Turned Upside Down*. Harmondsworth: Penguin.

Hill, Christopher (1990) *Antichrist*. London: Verso. Hobbes (1975 [1651]) Leviathan. Harmondsworth: Pelican.

Linebaugh (1991) *The London Hanged*. London: Verso.

Linebaugh (2000) *The Many-Headed Hydra*. London: Verso.

Maritain (2005 [1930]) *An Introduction To Philosophy*. London: Continuum.

McEnery, T. (2009) *Swearing in English: Bad Language, Purity and Power from 1586 to the Present*. London: Routledge.

Milbank, John (2014) *Beyond Secular Order: The Representation of Being and the Representation of the People*. Oxford: Wiley- Blackwell.

Milbank, John (2015) 'On the Paraethical: Gillian Rose and Political Nihilism' in *Telos* No.173 Gillian Rose special issue. Winter 2015.

Missac, Pierre (1995 [1987]) *Walter Benjamin's* Passages. Massachusets: MIT.

Murry, Middleton (1933) *William Blake*. Jonathan Cape.

Nietzsche (2004) *The Nietzsche Reader*. Harmondsworth: Penguin.

Osborne, Peter (2015) speaking at the *Gillian Rose: 20 year retrospective* day conference, Friday 9th of January, 2015, at Durham University's Lindisfarne Centre.

Osborne, Peter (2015) 'Gillian Rose and Marxism' in *Telos* No.173 Gillian Rose special issue. Winter 2015.

Parra, Nicanor (2004) Antipoems: *How to Look Better and Feel Great*. New York: New Directions.

Patocka, Jan et al (1977) *Charter 77*. Prague: Vaclav Havel Archives.

Paye, Jean-Claude (2015) '"The End of History" or Messianic Time' in *Telos* No.173 Gillian Rose special issue. Winter 2015.

Petrácek, Tomáš (2014) *Man, Values and the Dynamics of Medieval Society. Anthropological Concepts of the Middle Ages in a Transcultural Perspective*. Lublin: El-Press.

Petrácek, Tomáš (2014) *In the Maelstrom of Secularization, Collaboration and Persecution. Roman Catholicism in Modern Czech Society and the State*. Lublin: El-Press.

Pound, Marcus (2015) 'A Reader's Guide' in *Telos* No.173 Gillian Rose special issue. Winter 2015.

Raubach, Michael (2015) speaking at the *Gillian Rose: 20 year retrospective* day conference, Friday 9th of January, 2015, at Durham University's Lindisfarne Centre.

Rose, Gillian (1992) *The Broken Middle: Out of Our Ancient Society*. Oxford: Blackwell.

Rose, Gillian (1997) *Love's Work*. London: Vintage.

Shanks (2008) *Against Innocence: Gillian Rose's Reception and Gift of Faith*. Canterbury: SCM Press.

Shanks (2015) *Hegel versus 'Inter-Faith Dialogue': A General Theory of True Xenophilia*. Cambridge University Press.

Shanks, Andrew (2015) 'Gillian Rose and Theology: Salvaging Faith' in *Telos* No.173 Gillian Rose special issue. Winter 2015.

Wansbrough, Henry (1996) *An Introduction to the Pauline Letters*. This is an extremely important text for this work, written for the fourth of the annual courses on Scripture: Union of Monastic Superiors.

Ward, W.H. (1976) 'Mrs. Behn's "The Widow Ranter"' in the *South Atlantic Bulletin*, Vol. 41, No. 4. South Atlantic Modern Language Association.

First published in this edition by Boiler House Press, 2021
Part of UEA Publishing Project
Copyright © Steve Hanson, 2021

Cover Design and Typesetting by Louise Aspinall
Typeset in Arnhem Pro
Printed by Tallinn Book Printers
Distributed by NBN International

ISBN: 978-1-911343-74-5